My Weirder School #1

Miss Child Has Gone Wild!

Dan Gutman

Pictures by
Jim Paillot

HARPER
An Imprint of HarperCollinsPublishers

To Coleman and Oscar Burke

Miss Child Has Gone Wild!

Text copyright © 2011 by Dan Gutman

Illustrations copyright © 2011 by Jim Paillot

Library of Congress Cataloging-in-Publication Data

Gutman, Dan.

Miss Child has gone wild! / Dan Gutman ; pictures by Jim Paillot. — 1st ed.

p. cm. — (My weirder school ; #1)

Summary: A.J. and his fellow third graders from Ella Mentry School, including new student
Alexia, go on a field trip to the zoo, where they meet a very strange zookeeper.

ISBN 978-0-06-196917-1 (lib. bdg.) — ISBN 978-0-06-196916-4 (pbk. bdg.)

[1. Zoos—Fiction. 2. School field trips—Fiction. 3. Zoo keepers—Fiction. 4. Humorous
stories.] I. Paillot, Jim, ill. II. Title.

PZ7.G9846Mjc 2011   2010045634

[Fic]—dc22   CIP

                                                                                    AC

Typography by Joel Tippie

12   13   14   15   CG/BR   10 9 8 7

First Edition

Contents

We Win!

My name is A.J. and I hate school.

I don't even know why school was invented. Whoever thought up that idea was mean. Reading, writing, and math are way overrated. You can learn all you need to know just by watching TV. I'm talking about important stuff, like which breakfast cereal is crunchier and which video games let you shoot more bad guys.

If I was the president, the first thing I'd do would be to close all the schools and turn them into skate parks. That would be cool.*

My teacher is Mr. Granite, who is from another planet. He was about to start our math lesson when an announcement came over the loudspeaker. It was our principal, Mr. Klutz, who has no hair at all.

"The winner of the Cleanest Classroom in the School Contest goes to . . . Mr. Granite's third graders!"

---

* So, how's it going? Enjoying the book so far? Can we get you something to drink while you're reading? Or a pillow, maybe?

"Yay!" everybody in our class shouted.

"What do we win?" I asked Mr. Granite.

"You win a classroom that's clean," he said.

"For the rest of you," Mr. Klutz announced, "please be careful not to leave any food around your classroom. It attracts bugs and mice. We want to teach *students* at Ella Mentry School, not bugs and mice."

"I hate mice," said Mr. Granite.

"Why would *anyone* leave food around a classroom?" asked this annoying girl named Andrea Young with curly brown hair.

"That's disgusting," said Emily, this

crybaby girl who always agrees with everything Andrea says.

"Maybe they want to feed the bugs and mice," said my friend Ryan.

"Okay, it's time for math," said Mr. Granite. "Turn to page twenty-three in your—"

Mr. Granite didn't get the chance to finish his sentence, because at that very moment the weirdest thing in the history of the world happened.

A girl came into the class.

Well, that's not the weird part, because girls come into the class all the time. The weird part was that she *skateboarded* into the class!

The girl was wearing a backward

baseball cap

and a black T-shirt

that said LED ZEPPELIN on it.

"Yo!" she said as she hopped off her skateboard. "They told me I was supposed to be in Mr. Granite's class. Are you Mr. Granite?"

"Yes," Mr. Granite replied. "Who are you?"

"My name is A.J.," the girl said, "and I hate school."

WHAT?!

The New Girl

Everybody turned and looked at me when the girl named A.J. skateboarded into the class.

"Hey, the new girl is *cool*!" whispered my friend Michael, who sits behind me.

"What does A.J. stand for?" asked Mr. Granite. He was looking through his attendance list.

"Alexia Juarez," the girl said. "My family just moved here from Puerto Rico last week."

"Oooooh!" said Ryan. "The new girl has the same initials as A.J. They must be in *love*!"

"When are you and the new girl gonna get married?" asked Michael.

I felt my face getting hot. I looked around the class and spotted Andrea. She was looking at the new girl. Andrea had on a mean face, and her arms were crossed in front of her. When people cross their arms in front of them, it means they're mad. Nobody knows why.

"Do you *really* hate school, Alexia?" asked Emily.

"Sure I do," said Alexia. "School is something grown-ups invented so they wouldn't have to take care of us during the day."

Wow! The new girl was a lot like me, but a girl!

"I don't agree with that," Mr. Granite said, "but welcome to our class, Alexia. Take off your hat, please. We don't wear hats in school."

Alexia made a face but took off her hat anyway. She has blond hair. She shook her head. Her hair fell all the way down her back and swirled around in slow motion, just like in those shampoo commercials on TV.

"Oooooooooooooh!" everybody said.

"Your hair is pretty, Alexia," said Andrea.

What a brownnoser! Andrea probably wishes she had long blond hair.

"Maybe Alexia would like to tell us a little about herself," said Mr. Granite.

"Do you like to dance and sing?" asked Andrea.

"No," Alexia replied. "I like to play video games and ride my skateboard."

WHAT?! I like to play video games and ride my skateboard.

"Can you drop into a half-pipe on your skateboard?" I asked.

"Sure," Alexia said. "I do that all the time."

Wow! Even I can't drop into a half-pipe on a skateboard. That's scary.

"Do you like to play dress up?" asked Emily.

"No," Alexia replied. "I like to play football and eat pizza."

WHAT?! I like to play football and eat pizza!

"Do you like to play with dolls?" asked Andrea.

Alexia slapped her own head. "No!" she replied. "Dolls are yucky. I like to ride trick bikes."

WHAT?! I like to ride trick bikes!

"Do you like animals?" asked Neil, who we call the nude kid even though he wears clothes.

"Oh yes," Alexia said. "My favorite animal is the penguin."

WHAT?! I *love* penguins!

This was getting weird.

"I know what you are," Andrea said to Alexia. "You're a tomboy."

"That's right!" Alexia said proudly. "I am."

"Okay, take a seat over there, Alexia," said Mr. Granite. "You can sit next to A.J. Now, please open your math books to page twenty-three."

"Oooooh!" said Ryan. "The two A.J.s are sitting next to each other. They must be in *love*!"

"When are you gonna get married?" asked Michael.

If those guys weren't my best friends, I would hate them.

Miss Child
Is Weird

3

I opened my math book to page twenty-three. Alexia skateboarded over to the desk next to me and sat down. Then she leaned over so that her long blond hair was touching my desk.

"Yo, dude," she whispered in my ear. "You want a piece of gum?"

"We're not allowed to chew gum in school," I whispered back.

"Yeah, so?" Alexia said. She popped a piece of gum into her mouth.

Mr. Granite clapped his hands together. *Clap clap, clap-clap-clap.* "Okay!" he said. "Maybe now we can finally get to our math lesson."

I glanced sideways and saw that Alexia was writing something on a little scrap of paper. She folded it up and tossed it on my desk. I opened up the note. It said . . .

I HATE MATH

I turned the paper over and wrote on the other side . . .

ME TOO

Then I passed the paper back to Alexia.

"Mr. Granite," said Andrea, "the two A.J.s are passing notes back and forth."

"Don't be a tattletale, Andrea," said Mr. Granite.

"Oh, snap!" said Ryan.

Nah-nah-nah boo-boo on Andrea! In

her face! I was going to say something mean to her, but you'll never believe who poked their head into the door at that moment.

Nobody. Why would anyone poke their head into a door? That would hurt. But you'll never believe who poked their head into the door*way*.

It was a lady. She had something around her neck. And it wasn't a necklace.

It was a snake!

"EEEEEEEEEEEEEK!" screamed all the girls. "A snake!" They were all freaking out.

"I'm scared!" said Emily, who is scared of everything.

"Hello," the lady said. "I'm Miss Child, and I work at the zoo."

"Uh, we're in the middle of our math lesson right now," said Mr. Granite. "To what do we owe the pleasure of your company, Miss Child?"*

"Mr. Klutz said I could stop in and show the kids our newest friend at the zoo," said Miss Child. "We named him Pumpkin. Isn't he adorable?"

"No!" said all the girls.

I had to admit that Pumpkin *was* pretty adorable. But I wasn't about to say so, because I never say *anything* is adorable.

"Do you want to touch Pumpkin?"

---

* That's grown-up talk for "What are *you* doing here?"

asked Miss Child.

"No!" shouted all the girls.

"Yes!" shouted all the boys. Plus Alexia. We lined up to touch Pumpkin.

"Snakes are cool," said Alexia. "I saw snakes back home in Puerto Rico all the time."

I thought Pumpkin was going to be all slimy and disgusting, but he wasn't. He didn't bite me or anything.

Miss Know-It-All Andrea must have been jealous that Alexia liked snakes, because she started telling everybody all about them.

"Did you know that snakes are deaf?" said Andrea. "They pick up vibrations

through their jawbones. And they smell
with their tongues."

What a brownnoser.

"That's true, Andrea!" said Miss Child.
"Hey, do you kids want to see something
really cool?"

She reached into her pocket and pulled
out a big . . . hairy . . . spider!

"Ewwwwwwwwwwwwww!"

"This is my friend Melvin," said Miss Child. "He's a tarantula."

"You keep a tarantula in your *pocket*?" I asked. That was weird.

"Spiders are gross," said Neil the nude kid.

"I don't feel that way," Miss Child said. "At the zoo, we appreciate *all* living creatures, large and small, land creatures and sea creatures, meat eaters and plant eaters, creatures that fly or swim or crawl on their bellies and blah blah blah blah blah blah blah blah blah blah blah blah blah blah blah blah blah blah blah blah blah blah blah blah blah blah blah blah blah."

She went on and on, talking about how

great animals are and all that *Lion King* circle-of-life stuff. I thought I was gonna fall asleep. But then Miss Child said something that got my attention.

"I have big news," she said.

"Miss Child has a big nose," Alexia whispered in my ear.

"The *real* reason why I came here is because you have the cleanest class in the whole school," she said. "So your class has been chosen to go on a field trip . . . to the zoo!"

"Yay!" everybody shouted.

My Zoo Buddy

Field trips are cool because you get to leave school. The only field trips that aren't cool are the ones where they take you on a field trip to a *field*. Going to a field is lame.

The next day, everybody was excited about our trip to the zoo. My mom packed me a peanut butter and jelly sandwich for lunch. Emily brought in a camera so she could take pictures of the animals. We all had to turn in a sheet of paper our parents signed that said if we get attacked by a bear or something, our parents can't sue the zoo or the school.

While we were getting ready to leave for the field trip, Ms. Hannah, our art teacher, came into the class. She told us she would be coming along on the trip as our chaperone. In case you don't know French, a chaperone is a grown-up who tells everybody to stop talking. Ms. Hannah's art program was almost canceled because of budget cuts, so now she has to do other stuff besides teach art. Like go on field trips.

Mr. Granite told us that we would have to have a "zoo buddy" so we wouldn't get lost at the zoo.

"Yo, A.J., do you want to be my zoo buddy?" Alexia asked me.

I didn't know what to say. I didn't know what to do. I had to think fast. It would be cool to be zoo buddies with Alexia. But I knew the guys would make fun of me if I was zoo buddies with a girl.

I thought and thought. I thought so hard, I thought my head was going to explode.

In the end I didn't have to decide who

would be my zoo buddy. Mr. Granite did.

"Emily, you and Alexia will be zoo buddies," he said. "Michael and Ryan are zoo buddies. And A.J., you be zoo buddies with Andrea."

Ugh, disgusting!

Andrea looked at me with this big smile on her face.

"Arlo! You and I are going to be zoo buddies!" she said. She calls me by my real name because she knows I don't like it.

"Oooooh!" said Ryan. "A.J. and Andrea are zoo buddies. They must be in *love!*"

"When are you two zoo buddies gonna get married?" asked Michael.

Alexia was looking at Andrea. She had

on a mean face and
had her arms crossed in
front of her. She must have been
mad that Andrea was my zoo buddy. Or
maybe she just had to go to the bathroom.
"It's time to get on the bus," said Ms.

Hannah. "Single file, everyone."

"Don't forget to bring along your lunch," said Mr. Granite.

Alexia was the line leader, and she skateboarded down the ramp in front of the school. I guess she skateboards everywhere. The rest of us had to walk a million hundred miles to where the bus was parked.

"Bingle boo!" said Mrs. Kormel, our school bus driver. "Limpus kidoodle."

Mrs. Kormel doesn't talk like regular people. She invented her own secret language. Bingle boo means "hello." Limpus kidoodle means "sit down."

Mrs. Kormel is not normal.

We all piled onto the bus. I had to sit next to my zoo buddy, Andrea.

"Isn't this exciting, Arlo?" she asked. "Don't you just love field trips?"

Andrea was rubbing her hands together, which is what people do when they're excited

ELLA MENTRY SCHOOL

about something. Nobody knows why.

"No," I replied.

Andrea gets excited about everything. If a grown-up told her we were going to go outside and stare at a pile of dirt all day, she would be rubbing her hands together with excitement.

"I hope they have elephants at the zoo," Andrea told me. "Did you know that some elephants are thirteen feet tall and

weigh over fifteen thousand pounds?"

"Everybody knows that," I lied.

You should never let a know-it-all like Andrea know that she knows something you don't know. That's the first rule of being a kid.

"Elephants also spend up to sixteen hours a day eating," Andrea said.

"So does your face," I told her.

Andrea probably looked up elephants

in her encyclopedia at home. What is her problem? Why can't an elephant fall on her head?

I had to listen to Andrea tell me everything she knew about elephants for the whole bus ride. I thought I was gonna die.

Finally, after riding a million hundred miles, we got to the zoo.

Miss Child was waiting for us. She came over to the bus and led us to a room where we put our backpacks. Then she passed out name tags so she could pretend she knew our names when she talked to us.

"Do you have elephants at the zoo?" asked Little Miss I-Know-Everything-About-Elephants.

"Oh yes!" replied Miss Child.

Andrea jumped up and down with excitement, like she was opening her birthday presents.

"Before we start your tour," Miss Child said, "I want to talk to you for a few minutes about our zoo. We don't believe that animals should be locked up in cages. Blah blah blah blah blah. All our animals live in an environment that is made to resemble their natural habitat. Blah blah blah blah blah. We need to respect all living creatures. Blah blah blah blah blah. There is nothing separating you from the animals here. So you need to be careful at all times. Blah blah blah blah blah blah

blah blah blah blah blah when will this end blah blah blah blah blah blah blah please make her stop blah blah blah blah blah blah blah blah blah blah."

Miss Child talked for a million hundred minutes about how wonderful animals are. It was really boring. I just wanted to see some cool animals, not listen to some lady talk about them.

"I love animals," Miss Child finally said. "Do you love animals, too?"

Everybody except Emily raised a hand.

"I'm allergic to animals with fur," she said. "Dogs, cats, ferrets . . ."

That was true. One time Neil the nude kid brought his pet ferret Mr. Wiggles to school. It got out of its cage and was running around the school all day. By the time we found it in Emily's hat, we had voted Mr. Wiggles president of the school.

Emily is probably allergic to her own shadow.

Miss Child told us to go around in a circle and tell something about our pets.

"I have a dog named Buttons," I said when it was my turn.

"Tell us something interesting about Buttons, A.J.," said Miss Child.

There really wasn't anything interesting to say about Buttons. He was just a plain old dog. But I had to say *something*.

"Well," I said, "sometimes Buttons poops

on the floor."

Everybody laughed because I said "poop." If you ever want to make somebody laugh, just go up to them and say "poop." It works every time. Nobody knows why.

"Ooh, that's too bad that your dog poops on the floor," said Miss Child. "What does your mother do?"

"She poops in the bathroom," I said. "Duh!"

Everybody laughed even though I didn't say anything funny.

Next it was Andrea's turn.

"After school I earn money by dog sitting," she said.

"You sit on *dogs*?" I asked. "That's weird!

Why would anyone want to sit on a dog?"

"I don't sit on dogs, Arlo!" Andrea told me. "I take care of dogs when their owners aren't home. It's like babysitting."

"You sit on babies too?" I said. "Isn't that against the law?"

Andrea got all mad. I knew that she didn't sit on dogs or babies. But it's fun to yank her chain.

5

Binky the Elephant

Finally it was time for us to explore the zoo.

"We don't want anyone to get lost," said Miss Child. "So everyone hold hands with your zoo buddy."

Andrea looked at me and held out her hand.

"Hold my hand, Arlo," she said, smiling.

"No way," I said. "I'm not holding your hand."

"You have to. Miss Child said so."

I looked at Miss Child. She gave me one of those grown-up looks. I held Andrea's hand.

Ugh, disgusting!

Alexia had to hold hands with crybaby Emily. She didn't look too happy about it. Michael had to hold hands with Ryan. They didn't like it either. Nobody likes holding hands. That's the first rule of being a kid.

"Would you like to go visit Elephant Alley?" asked Miss Child.

"Yeah!" everybody said. Even Mr. Granite and Ms. Hannah were excited to see the elephants.

"I love elephants!" said Andrea.

"Then why don't you marry one?" I told her.

We all followed Miss Child to Elephant Alley. Two elephants were lumbering around. They were cool. Everybody was oohing and ahhing. There was a big ditch that separated the people from the elephants so they couldn't charge us and step on our heads and trample us to death.

"This is Winky and Binky," said Miss Child. "They come from Thailand. Some elephants are thirteen feet tall and weigh over fifteen thousand pounds."

"See, I told you," Andrea whispered in my ear.

Miss Child climbed over the ditch and

jumped right into Elephant Alley.

"Isn't that dangerous to be so close to the elephants?" asked Mr. Granite.

"Not at all," Miss Child replied. "The animals are our friends. We should love all living creatures. Blah blah blah blah blah."

She went over to a shed and took out a big easel and some buckets and paint-brushes. She dipped a brush into one of the buckets and put it in Binky's trunk.

"What's he doing?" asked Emily.

"Binky likes to paint," Miss Child said. "It relaxes him."

"That's ridiculous," said Ms. Hannah. "Elephants can't paint."

Ms. Hannah knows a lot about art, so I figured she was right. But then the most amazing thing in the history of the world happened. Binky took the paint-brush, pressed it against the paper on the easel, and drew a thick blue line all by himself.

"WOW," we all said, which is MOM upside down. None of us thought an elephant would be able to do that.

Binky carefully painted another line that crossed over the first line. Everybody was oohing and ahhing.

"Maybe elephants *can* paint," said Ms. Hannah. "How does he do that?"

"Elephants have more than 40,000 muscles in their trunk," said Miss Child as she dipped Binky's brush into the bucket of paint for him.

Binky painted more lines on the easel. Some of them were straight, and some of them were curvy. It looked like he was actually trying to draw a picture of something.

"What's he painting?" asked Andrea.

"It looks like a picture of an elephant!" shouted Michael.

"It's a self-portrait!" said Ms. Hannah. "He's painting *himself*! It's beautiful!"

She was right! With a few more lines, Binky the elephant had painted a picture of an elephant. It was the most amazing thing in the history of the world! We all clapped when he dropped the brush on the ground and lumbered away from the easel.*

"What does the zoo do with those

---

* Want to see elephants paint for real? Go to: www.elephantart.com/catalog/homepage.php.

paintings?" asked Ms. Hannah.

"Oh, we just throw them away," said Miss Child.

"May I keep that one as a souvenir?" Ms. Hannah asked.

"Certainly," Miss Child said. She took the paper off the easel and climbed over the ditch so she could hand it to Ms. Hannah.

"This painting is *priceless*!" Ms. Hannah whispered to us excitedly.

"You mean it isn't worth anything?" I asked.

"Just the opposite, A.J.," Ms. Hannah told me. "I think Binky could be the next Picasso! This is a rare masterpiece! It could be worth *millions* of dollars!"

"Really?" we all said.

"I bet I could sell this to an art dealer," Ms. Hannah said, "and if I donated the money to the school, I could save the art program!"

Wow, Ms. Hannah should get the No bell prize for that one. That's a prize they give out to people who don't have bells.

Lulu the Gorilla

"Let's go meet the gorillas!" Miss Child said excitedly.

She led us over a little wooden bridge to an area called Gorilla Gardens. There was a concrete wall like the inside of a swimming pool that curved down to where a gorilla was sitting. It was swatting flies and making grunting noises. It looked scary.

Miss Child slid down the concrete wall on her bottom.

"Isn't it dangerous to be so close to a gorilla?" Emily asked.

"Of course not," said Miss Child. "Gorillas are almost like humans. They share nearly ninety-eight percent of our DNA. Gorillas are our friends. Blah blah blah blah blah. This is my friend Lulu."

Miss Child put her hands in front of Lulu's face and moved her fingers around.

"What are you doing?" asked Mr. Granite.

"I'm talking with Lulu," said Miss Child.

"Lulu understands sign language?" I said. "That is cool!"

"Miss Child is sort of like Dr. Doolittle," said Michael. "She can talk with the animals just like him."

"Lulu is very smart," Miss Child told us. "She understands more than a thousand words."

"That's more than some kids I know," said Andrea.

"Oh, snap!" said Ryan.

Lulu made some signs with her hands.

"What did she say?" asked Alexia.

"Lulu says she wants to tell you kids a joke," translated Miss Child.

"I like jokes," said Alexia.

Lulu made some more signs with her hands.

"What did she say?" asked Neil the nude kid.

"Lulu asked, 'Why did the raisin go out with the prune?'" said Miss Child.

"Why?" we all asked.

Lulu made some signs.

"Because he couldn't find a date," translated Miss Child.

We all groaned.

"I don't get it," said Emily.

"That's a dumb joke," I said.

Lulu made some more signs with her hands.

"Lulu wants to tell you another joke," translated Miss Child.

Lulu made some signs.

"What did she say?" asked Michael.

"Lulu asked, 'What's the difference between roast beef and pea soup?'" translated Miss Child.

"What?" we all asked.

Lulu made some signs.

"You can roast beef," Miss Child translated, "but you can't pea soup."

We all groaned.

"I don't get it," said Emily.

"Lulu's jokes are lame," I said.

Lulu stood up and started to grunt loudly and stamp her feet.

"Why is she doing that?" asked Andrea.

"Lulu is mad because you kids didn't laugh at her jokes," Miss Child told us.

"That's because her jokes are terrible," said Ryan.

"You should have laughed at them anyway," Miss Child told us. "You hurt Lulu's feelings."

"Gorillas have feelings?" asked Neil the nude kid.

"Of course they do," said Miss Child.

"All living creatures have feelings, and blah blah blah blah blah . . . "

Lulu started making signs really fast to Miss Child.

"What did she say?" asked Neil the nude kid.

"Lulu says children are stupid," translated Miss Child.

"Oh, snap!" said Ryan.

"Stupid is not a nice word," said Andrea. "We're not supposed to say stupid."

"If you ask me," I said, "Lulu shouldn't blame us just because her jokes are lame."

"Yeah," said Michael, "she should learn some funnier jokes."

"I think Lulu is just in a bad mood

today," said Miss Child.

Lulu started making more signs with her fingers. Mr. Granite and Ms. Hannah tried to put their hands over our eyes so we couldn't see.

"Don't look, kids!" said Mr. Granite.

"What is Lulu saying?" I asked as I tried to pull Mr. Granite's hands off my eyes.

"I can't tell you," Miss Child said. "It's inappropriate for children."

I think I saw Lulu make a sign that my dad once made to some guy in a car who cut in front of him on the highway.

"Lulu is using bad words!" said Andrea.

"I think Lulu is cursing in sign language," said Alexia.

"That's not very nice," said Emily.

"Lulu should watch her language," said Andrea.

We wanted to stick around and find out what Lulu was saying, but Mr. Granite and Ms. Hannah told us we had to get out of there and go see some of the other animals.

Gorillas are weird.

The Truth About Miss Child

7

We walked all over the zoo and saw a bunch of other animals—birds, snakes, walruses, alligators, monkeys. Animals are cool.

"Did you know that there are more than a million species of animals on Earth?" said my zoo buddy Andrea.

She is so annoying. Little Miss Know-It-All had to read every sign about every animal so she can go home and show her parents how smart she is.

Soon it was time for lunch. We walked back to the room where we left our backpacks. Everybody took out a lunch box, except for one person.

Me.

"Where's my lunch?" I said to Ms. Hannah.

"Your lunch is wherever you left it, A.J.," she told me.

I hate when grown-ups say that.

"Arlo must have left his lunch back at school," said Andrea. "I guess he wasn't paying attention when Mr. Granite told us to be sure to take our lunch with us."

"I wasn't paying attention to your *face*," I told Andrea.

All the kids sat at a long picnic table to eat their lunch. Mr. Granite and Ms. Hannah sat at another table for grown-ups. Miss Child said she would get me a sandwich from the zoo cafeteria. She said I could have a turkey or tuna sandwich.

"Do you have turkeys or tuna in the zoo?" I asked. It would be weird to eat a sandwich made from an animal they have running around the zoo.

"We have turkeys in the zoo," Miss Child said.

"Then I'll have a tuna sandwich," I told
her.

Miss Child ran out and came back with
a tuna sandwich and a carton of milk for
me.

"I'll be back in a few minutes," she told
us. "I promised the baboons that I
would eat lunch with them
today."

"Miss Child is weird," Alexia said when she left.

"Yeah, I think she loves animals a little too much," said Michael.

"Maybe she's not a zookeeper at all," I said. "Did you ever think of that?"

"What do you mean?" asked Emily.

"Well," I said, "maybe Miss Child kidnapped the real zookeeper and is just *pretending* to be a zookeeper because she's obsessed with animals."

"Stop trying to scare Emily," said Andrea.

"I'm scared!" said Emily.

"Maybe Miss Child locked the *real* zookeeper in a cage filled with poisonous rattlesnakes," said Alexia. "Stuff like that happens all the time, you know."

"We've got to *do* something!" shouted Emily, and then she ran out of the room.

Sheesh! Get a grip! That girl will fall for anything. After Emily ran away, Alexia gave me a high-five, and Andrea gave me a mean face.

Penguin Paradise

Mr. Granite and Ms. Hannah went to find Emily. Miss Child came back from her lunch with the baboons. She said that after we finished eating, it was "Free Zoo Time." We could go wherever we wanted in the zoo as long as we held hands with our zoo buddy. Miss Child said she would be Alexia's zoo buddy until Emily got back.

"I want to look at the reptiles!" said Neil the nude kid.

"I want to look at the birds!" said Michael.*

"I want to look at the tigers!" said Ryan.

All the kids ran out of the room to go look at animals.

"What do *you* want to look at, Arlo?" Andrea asked me.

There was only one animal I wanted to look at. My favorite animal in the whole world.

Penguins.

---

* You don't have to go to a zoo to look at birds. Just look up in the sky.

Andrea and I had to walk about a million hundred miles to Penguin Paradise. She was holding my hand the whole time. Ugh, disgusting!

"Arlo, if we were married," Andrea said as we walked along the path, "we would hold hands like this all the time. Holding hands is so romantic."

I thought I was gonna throw up.

"Can I ask you a question, Arlo?" Andrea said.

"You just did," I told her.

"Do you like that new girl Alexia better than me?" Andrea asked.

"No!" I said. "I mean, yes! I mean . . ."

The truth was that I didn't like Alexia better than Andrea. And I didn't like Andrea better than Alexia. I didn't like *either* of them. I didn't like *any* girls. Girls are yucky. Except for my mom. She's not yucky. But I'll bet she was yucky when she was a girl. Because all girls are yucky.

Finally we got to Penguin Paradise. There were penguins *everywhere*. Hundreds of them. They were waddling around, jumping in the water and swimming. It was cool.

I pressed my nose against the glass. Ever since I was a baby, I loved penguins. I had a stuffed penguin in my crib. On Halloween one year, I dressed up like a penguin. I saw that movie *March of the Penguins* about ten times. I *love* penguins!

Looking at all those penguins walking

around, it was like I was hypnotized. It almost seemed like they were talking to me.

"Come with us, A.J.!" one of the penguins seemed to whisper in my ear. "We'll go to Antarctica!"

"Kids don't have to go to school in Antarctica," whispered a second penguin.

"No teachers," whispered another penguin.

"No parents," whispered another.

"Best of all, no Andrea," whispered another penguin.

"Come with us and live in peace," another penguin whispered to me. "We'll slide around on the ice all day. It will be penguin paradise."

"I'm coming," I told the penguins. "I want to be with you . . ."

Suddenly I felt something grabbing the back of my shirt. It was Andrea's hand.

"Arlo, are you okay?" she asked. "You started climbing into the penguin pool! It looked like you were in a daze. Who were you talking to?"

"Uh, nobody," I said.

That was weird!

Suddenly Miss Child and Alexia came running over. They looked all upset.

"What's wrong?" Andrea asked.

"Emily is still missing!" Miss Child said. "We can't find her *anywhere*!"

In Search of Emily

We looked all over the zoo for Emily. We looked in Turtle Town, Alligator Avenue, Lizard Lane, Rhino Road, Bat Boulevard, Zebra Zone, Snake Street, and Hedgehog Highway. We searched the bathrooms, the snack bars, and the gift shop. No Emily.

"Emily!" we shouted. "Where are you?"

Miss Child, Mr. Granite, and Ms. Hannah looked really upset. If Emily was gone forever, the grown-ups would be in big trouble. There were security guards with walkie-talkies hunting for Emily.

An announcement came over the zoo loudspeaker.

"If your name is Emily and you are lost, please report to the zoo office."

It was almost time to get back on the bus to go home. Emily was nowhere to be found. We had run out of places to look for her. The whole class gathered near the snack bar.

"What are we going to do?" asked Andrea. She looked like she might cry. "Emily is my best friend."

"Maybe she was eaten by a killer whale," I suggested.

"We don't have killer whales at the zoo," said Miss Child.

"Maybe she was eaten by a mongoose," said Michael.

"A mongoose isn't big enough to swallow a whole person," said Mr. Granite.

"What if the mongoose cut Emily up into little pieces first?" asked Ryan.

"Mongooses don't have knives!" said Ms. Hannah.*

"Maybe she was eaten by an elephant," said Neil the nude kid.

"Can we please stop that kind of talk?" said Miss Child. "The animals at the zoo are kind and gentle. None of them would ever eat a child and blah blah blah blah blah."

"Besides," said Andrea, "elephants are plant eaters. They eat grasses, leaves, fruit, and bark."

"Why would anyone want to eat a

---

* Or is that "mongeese"?

plant?" I said. "You should water plants, not eat them."

"Quiet, Arlo!" said Andrea. "This is serious! We have to find Emily."

"Eating plants is weird," I added.

"I feel terrible about this," said Miss Child. "It's all my fault. You kids were under my supervision."

"You have super vision?" I asked. "Cool!"

"Miss Child can see through walls!" said Michael.

"If you have super vision," said Neil the nude kid, "why don't you use it to find Emily?"

"Supervision means being in charge, dumbheads," said Andrea.

"Oh," I said. "I knew that."

"This is all *my* fault," said Mr. Granite. "Emily is my student. I should know where my students are at all times."

"No, it's my fault," said Ms. Hannah. "I'm the chaperone. I should have been watching her."

I love it when grown-ups argue over

whose fault something was. At least if they all think the thing that went wrong is their fault, nobody can say it was *my* fault.

Suddenly, I heard a voice calling in the distance.

"Help! Help!"

"That's Emily's voice!" yelled Andrea.

"Where is it coming from?" yelled Miss Child.

"Over there!" yelled Alexia.

"Where?" we all yelled.

"Lion Lane!"

Brian
the Lion

We all ran over to Lion Lane like we were in the Olympics. Alexia rode her skateboard, so she got there first.

"There she is!" Alexia shouted.

Lion Lane is another one of those areas in the zoo that has a concrete wall that curves down to where the animals live.

I leaned over the edge and looked down. There was Emily, lying on the ground at the bottom.

"Help!" Emily whimpered.

A big lion was pacing back and forth about ten feet away from Emily. It looked like the lion didn't even notice she was in there.

"Stay calm, Emily!" said Mr. Granite.

As if *anybody* could stay calm when they're trapped with a lion. I mean, Emily is a big crybaby, of course. But if I was stuck down at the bottom of Lion Lane, I would probably be freaking out and crying too.

"What is the lion's name?" asked Ms. Hannah.

"His name is Brian," said Miss Child.

"Brian the lion?" we all said.

"Brian," shouted Michael, "don't eat Emily!"

"Lions don't understand English, dumbhead," I told Michael.

"Can you climb out, Emily?" asked Mr. Granite.

"No!" Emily said. "I hurt my leg."

"We'll get you out of there, Emily!" shouted Miss Child.

"How did you get down there in the first place?" asked Ms. Hannah.

"I was taking a picture with my camera," Emily said. "I took a step backward and . . ." Emily couldn't finish the sentence because she started crying.

A bunch of kids suddenly remembered they brought cameras with them. They all started taking pictures of Emily and Brian the lion. It was a real Kodak moment.

Suddenly, Brian the lion walked over to Emily and started sniffing her.

"Brian the lion is going to eat Emily!" whispered Neil the nude kid.

"Do lions eat people?" whispered Ryan.

"Only under certain conditions," said Miss Child.

"Like what conditions?" whispered Andrea.

"Like when they're hungry," said Miss Child.

"We've got to *do* something!" said Andrea.

"Pretend to be dead, Emily!" shouted Miss Child. "We'll figure out a way to rescue you."

Emily pretended to be dead. Brian the lion was still sniffing her. Then Emily sneezed and Brian the lion jumped back.

"I think I'm allergic to lions," Emily said.

"That's the least of your problems," I told her.

"Maybe Brian the lion is allergic to Emily too," said Neil the nude kid.

Brian the lion went back to Emily and sniffed her some more. Emily sneezed again.

"Help!" she cried. "Do something! He's going to eat me!"

"I'll take care of this," said Miss Child.

She ran over to a little shed next to Lion Lane and came out with a long whip in one hand and a chair in her other hand. Then she went to the edge of Lion Lane and slid down the curved wall to the bottom. Brian the lion turned away from Emily and looked at Miss Child.

"Be a good boy, Brian," Miss Child said as she walked toward him slowly, holding the chair in front of her. "Leave Emily alone."

"Miss Child has gone wild," said Ryan.

"Isn't that dangerous, being so close to

a lion?" asked Mr. Granite.

"Don't be silly," Miss Child said. "The animals are my friends. We're all just living creatures trying to make our way in the world. We're all part of the family of man blah blah blah blah blah."

"Aren't you afraid that Brian the lion is

going to eat you?" asked Ms. Hannah.

"Brian wouldn't do that," Miss Child said. "I respect him and he respects me."

Brian the lion took a few steps toward Miss Child and growled at her. She cracked the whip and walked backward.

"Down, boy!" Miss Child said calmly.

It was cool. Miss Child was like a lion tamer in the circus. Emily was still lying on the ground, freaking out.

"Why don't you use your super vision to burn a hole in Brian the lion?" I yelled.

Brian the lion took a few more steps toward Miss Child. Then he growled and swiped at her with his paw.

"Ooooooooooooooh!" we all went.

"Don't worry," Miss Child said. "That's how Brian shows his respect for me."

"If he respects you so much," I said, "why do you need the whip and chair?"

That's when the weirdest thing in the history of the world happened. Brian the lion got up on his hind legs, growled really loudly, and started chasing Miss Child!

Miss Child dropped the

whip and chair and took off like she was in the Olympics. It was amazing!

"Help! Help!" shouted Miss Child.

"Run!" we all screamed. "Run for your life!"

Brian the lion was chasing Miss Child all over Lion Lane! And we got to see it live and in person. You should have been there!

Miss Child sure is a fast runner. If you ask me, they should use lions in the Olympics, because people run a lot faster when a lion is chasing them. Especially a hungry one.

While Brian the lion was chasing Miss Child around, Emily struggled to her feet and started limping toward the wall. She tried to climb up.

"You can do it, Emily!" shouted Andrea.

"I can't!" Emily shouted back. "It's too steep!"

That's when the most amazing thing in the history of the world happened.

But I'm not going to tell you what it is.

Okay, okay, I'll tell you. But you have to read the next chapter. So nah-nah-nah boo-boo on you.

The Amazing Surprise Ending!

Brian the lion was chasing Miss Child around Lion Lane like they were both in the Olympics. Emily was trying to climb the wall to get out of there. The rest of us were yelling and screaming and freaking out. Except for one person.

Alexia.

"I'm going in there," Alexia suddenly announced. "I'm going to get Emily."

"WHAT?!" I said. "How are you going to do that?"

Alexia took her skateboard and hung the front wheels over the edge of the concrete wall.

"This is a lot like the half-pipe at a skate park I used to go to," she said. "I'm going to skate down there and grab her."

"Are you crazy?" Andrea shouted. "You'll get killed!"

Alexia got up on her skateboard, leaned forward, and dropped into Lion Lane. She skated down the wall, picking up speed, and then skated up the wall on the opposite side. Then she spun around in the air and skated back down the wall. She's a really good skateboarder. It was like watching the X Games!

"Hold on, Emily!" Alexia shouted. "Here I come!"

Alexia skated right past Brian the lion and Miss Child. Then she crouched down on her board, reached out, and scooped Emily up in her arms. You should have seen it! It was the most amazing thing in the history of the world.

"WOW!" we all shouted, which is MOM upside down.

Brian the lion was still chasing Miss Child. Alexia and Emily were both on

the skateboard now, going back and forth
from one wall to the other like it was a
half-pipe.

"Help!" Emily screamed. "I don't know how to skateboard!"

"But I do!" yelled Alexia.

They kept going back and forth, up one wall and down the other. Finally, they built up enough speed to reach the top of the wall. Mr. Granite and Ms. Hannah reached over and grabbed them, pulling them up to the top.

Everybody was hugging Emily and telling Alexia how great she was at skateboarding. Andrea was standing at the side with a mean face and her arms crossed in front of her. I guess she was mad because Alexia was a big hero.

We looked back down into Lion Lane.

Brian the lion was still chasing Miss Child around. Just as he was about to grab her, she climbed up the wall. We all leaned over to pull her up to the top. Miss Child lay down on the grass. She was all out of breath and her hair was messed up.

"Are you okay, Miss Child?" asked Andrea. "Brian the lion almost ate you!"

"No, no," she replied. "Brian just needed a little exercise. He's a gentle creature. He wouldn't hurt a fly. Blah blah blah blah blah."

In the distance, we heard the honk of a school bus.

"Bingle boo!" shouted our bus driver, Mrs. Kormel. It was time to go.

She was really tired from all that running, but Miss Child walked us over to the bus to say good-bye.

"Well, I hope you enjoyed your visit to the zoo," she said. "And I hope it gave you kids a new appreciation for all the living creatures on earth blah blah blah blah blah. Come visit us again real soon."

"We will!" we all shouted.

On the bus, everybody was talking about the exciting things we saw at the zoo—Binky the artistic elephant, Lulu the angry gorilla, and Brian the lion who almost ate Emily and Miss Child. We all agreed that when our parents came to pick us up and asked us what we did at the zoo, we would all say "Nothing."*

Mr. Granite fell asleep on the bus ride home. Mrs. Kormel talked to us in her secret language. Ms. Hannah carefully rolled up Binky the elephant's priceless painting so she could sell it and save the art program.

After a million hundred hours, we finally arrived at school. We had to go back to our classroom to get our stuff.

And you'll never believe what was sitting on my desk when we walked in the door.

I'm not going to tell you.

---

* Even if you almost get eaten by a lion, when your parents ask what happened during the day, always say, "Nothing." That's the first rule of being a kid.

Okay, okay, I'll tell you.

It was a mouse!

"EEEEEEEEEEEEEEK!" screamed all the girls.

"There's a mouse on A.J.'s desk!" Emily shrieked. "Ewwww, disgusting!"

"You left your lunch in the class, Arlo!" Andrea said angrily. "It attracted mice! It's all your fault!"

"I guess we're not going to win Cleanest Class in the School this week," I admitted.

The mouse was sitting on my desk eating what was left of my peanut butter and jelly sandwich. Suddenly, the mouse looked up and saw us all staring at it. It jumped off my desk.

"EEEEEEEEEEEEEEK!" everybody screamed.

The mouse started running around the room, jumping on people's chairs and climbing on people's shoes. Everybody freaked out. Ms. Hannah got a broom from the closet and started chasing the mouse around the room with it. Mr. Granite grabbed the fire extinguisher off the wall and was running around, spraying the fire extinguisher all over the place. The rest of us were yelling and screaming.

"Stop!" Andrea yelled. "Mice are living creatures too. Just like the animals in the zoo! They should be treated with respect and dignity!"

"No they shouldn't!" I shouted.

"Kill it! Kill the mouse!" shouted Michael.

"KILL-THE-MOUSE!" everybody started chanting. "KILL-THE-MOUSE!"

Kids were throwing pens and pencils and erasers at the mouse. Mr. Granite put down the fire extinguisher and picked up the rolled-up painting that Binky the elephant made. He chased the mouse around the room, swinging the painting like a baseball bat.

"Stop!" Ms. Hannah shouted. "You're destroying our priceless painting!"

"I hate mice!" Mr. Granite hollered.

Eventually, the mouse must have gotten tired of running around our class, because it

jumped out the window.

It was all pretty hilarious. And we got to
see it live and in person.

So that's pretty much what happened.
Maybe the next time we go on a field
trip, I'll remember to bring my lunch.
Maybe Alexia and Andrea will stop cross-
ing their arms and making mean faces at
each other. Maybe Miss Child will stop
carrying tarantulas around in her pock-
ets. Maybe Binky the elephant will paint
another masterpiece for Ms. Hannah
to sell. Maybe Lulu the gorilla will stop
cursing kids out in sign language. Maybe
Emily will be more careful when she's

taking pictures. Maybe Mr. Granite will finally be able to get through a math lesson. Maybe the mouse will go to the zoo, where it will be treated with respect and dignity. Maybe my dog will stop pooping on the floor. Maybe Miss Child will stop saying blah blah blah blah blah all the time. Maybe our class will win another field trip to the zoo.

But it won't be easy!

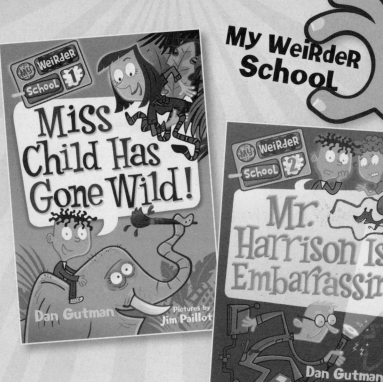